Boot Hill
Book 3
Reckoning

Luis Antwoord

Boot Hill: Reckoning
Copyright © 2015 by OÜ FOSSA

Standing on the boardwalk in front of the store owned by his new wife, Deborah, Issac watches a couple of dusty cowhands ride by on tired horses. The star on his chest that reads "Deputy" shines brightly in the midday sunlight. A phantom itch in his missing right arm makes him reach to scratch it with his left hand, but he only succeeds in scratching his ribs for what seems like the hundredth time. That sure does get annoying. He turns and strolls toward the jailhouse, his boots thumping hollowly on the boardwalk.

He still can't believe that he is married to Deborah, a short, stout woman who runs a small sewing store, but he is glad that he did. She has given him a new outlook on life, and a reason to live after his daughter was killed. The thought of his daughter makes him remember the horrors he faced in the last few months at the hands of the Irons Gang. They're gone now though, and the world's a better place because of it. Issac sees movement out of the corner of his eye. He spins around, his hand falling to the butt of his gun. Sam Tiller, the founder and unofficial mayor of Jericho, is rushing toward him, his face red from the exertion of moving his heavy body so fast.

"Where's the fire, Sam?" Issac asks with a grin, his hand falling away from his gun butt.

Sam hurries up to him, but he can't speak at first because he is breathing so hard. Issac, with a smile on his face, waits for him to catch his breath.

"Issac." Sam takes another gulp of air. "We've got trouble."

Issac's smile disappears instantly. "What is it, Sam?"

Sam finally catches his breath, but he is still

flushed, with sweat is pouring down his face. He looks at Issac for a moment before speaking.

"The Collins family is coming to town."

"You mean that family from Missouri who ran with the Bald Nobbers?"

"The very one."

"Why in the hell would they be coming to Jericho, Sam?"

"It seems that one of Irons' riders was a son to the old man, and now the whole family is coming to get revenge for his death."

"How in the hell did they find out?"

"One of the men who left Red sent a telegram to them over the wire that their boy had been killed and who done it."

"Son of a bitch." Issac sifts over what he knows about the Collins family, and none of it is good. "When will they be here?"

"They'll be here in a day, Issac." Sam looks him square in the eyes, and Issac can see that there is no run in the man. He might be scared, but he isn't going to run. "What are you going to do?"

"I'll meet 'em when they ride into town and tell them that I was the one that killed their kin."

"You know they'll gun you down right there."

"No, they won't, Sam." Issac turns and starts up the street, but he stops and turns back around. "Besides, I'm a hell of a lot harder to kill than that. Not a man of the law they won't. The old man is a feuding type, but he ain't no fool. He knows that the world is changing, and if he guns down a deputy the whole state will be after him and his kin. No, I suspect he'll try to get me angry and make me draw first."

"I'll stand with you when you go out to meet 'em, Issac."

"I appreciate that, Sam." Issac holds out a hand and Sam shakes it. "I've got some business to attend to, but I'll talk to you later."

He turns and walks up the street, his mind working over what he knows about the Collins family. Brent Collins is the father and an old bull of the woods. He's accustomed to people doing what he says because they're scared of him. He's hell on wheels from any distance with that Sharps .50 he carries. He's got five sons, and two of them are twins, Cain and Abel, who have both made a name for themselves as gunmen. They always work together, and they're as fast as lightning. They have a couple cousins too, but I'm not sure how many. The more he thinks about the Collins family, the more he realizes that he isn't going to be able to handle them on his own. As much as he hates to ask for help, he knows he is going to have to wire his cousin in San Francisco.

Turning on his heel, he makes his way over to the post office. Inside, he finds Ben Crawford lounged back in a chair with his feet propped up on a desk. The room is hot in the midday heat. When Ben sees him, he sits forward, the front legs of his chair thumping against the floor, as he spits a long stream of tobacco into a spittoon sitting six feet away. He turns to Issac with a grin, his teeth stained from tobacco.

"Ain't missed that spittoon in 15 years." He

tips his hat back on his head. "What can I do you for, Issac?"

"I need to send a wire, Ben."

Ben grabs a pen and a piece of paper off of his cluttered desk and clears a spot so his can write. He licks the end of the pen and looks up at Issac.

"Where to and what do you want it to say?"

"It needs to go to San Francisco. I want it to read: To the care of Harlow Douglas, stop. I've gotten myself into trouble, stop. I need your help, stop. It's the Collins family, stop. Signed, Issac O'Connor."

Ben writes down the telegram, but when Issac mentions the Collins family, his hand hesitates for a moment. He finishes the telegram with a flourish of his pen. He gets up and walks over to the counter with the telegram on it, but he doesn't send the message right away.

"The Collins family is coming here?"

"Coming here and looking to hang my hide."

Issac doesn't want to get into another

conversation about how mean they are; he already knows, so he tips his hat to Ben and walks out without another word. Walking up the street, he heads to the jailhouse. I better warn Henry about what's coming and tell him to stay out of it. There isn't any sense in him being killed over something I done. He finds Henry sitting on the porch of the jailhouse, eating chicken his wife cooked for his dinner.

"Sit down, Issac." He motions to the other chair on the porch with a drumstick. "There's a plenty. Sharon fixed some for you too."

"Thanks, Henry, but I ain't hungry right now."

Henry can see the look in his eyes, so he asks Issac what the problem is. Issac explains to him about what he heard and the telegram he sent to his cousin. He warns Henry that when the Collins family comes, they'll be coming for blood. Issac tells him to just stay out of it, but Henry raises his hand and stops him.

"I'm the Sheriff of this town, and I'll be damned if I'm going to stand by and watch a bunch of low-down murderers come in and take one of the citizens I've sworn to protect, especially one that is a friend. I'll stand with you when you go to meet 'em, Issac."

"I appreciate that, Henry."

An hour later, Issac is sitting behind the counter of his wife's store and listening to her yell at him. She keeps telling him that they need to leave, but he won't do it. It just isn't in his nature to run when the cards are down. When things get bad, he has always put his head down and bulled his way in with his fists swinging. Now you've just got one to swing. He grins despite himself. He doesn't like trouble, but somewhere deep inside he is a warrior who loves the thrill of battle. He figures that he would have been right at home in one of those gladiator arenas, just like in the books he's read about the Romans.

"And what that hell are you smiling about, Issac? They're coming to kill you."

"I think they'll find that I don't die so easy, honey. Now calm down before your heart quits."

"Calm down!" Her face flushes red with anger. "We haven't been married a month and you're already trying to get yourself killed."

Issac argues with her for a while, and eventually gets her to calm down and understand that he can't run. Deborah wraps him in a hug, and he hugs her back, as he knows that this may be the last time he gets to. Suddenly, a thought hits him. How did Sam know about the Collins family in the first place?

"Debbie?" Issac holds her arm and look into her eyes. "I've got to go find Sam and ask him a few questions. I'll be back shortly."

She stands on her tiptoes to give him a kiss. "You be careful, Issac O'Connor."

"Yes, ma'am."

Issac hurries out of the store and across the street to the post office. The sound of a buckboard coming across the bridge stops him. He turns to see an older man sitting tall in the driver's seat with 10 tall men riding horses around him. Oh hell. They're already here. The older man sees him and points a finger. Two of the riders spur their horses and ride straight for him. He plants his feet and places his hand on his gun butt.

The sun beats down on him, with sweat rolling down his back, as he stands in the street, alone, watching the two riders bear down on him. One rider veers off and stops in front of the post office, cutting off his escape in that direction. The other rides behind him, cutting off that exit. The buckboard pulls up in a cloud of dust, and the old man steps down with a Sharps .50 in his gnarled hands. By the way he carries it, there can be no mistake it's Brent. Behind the old man, two men step down and fan out left and right. They look identical to Issac. Cain and Abel. Brent's voice booms in the otherwise silent street.

"Are you Issac O'Connor?"

"I am." Issac touches a tongue to his lips and makes up his mind. When the shooting starts, I'll take Brent and the twins with me. I can at least get that many.

"I'm here on . . . "

"I know why you're here, and you're a fool if you think I'm just gonna let you take hang me."

Brent's face flares red with anger. "I WILL KILL YOU, O'CONNOR!"

"You might, but not today." A voice comes from the post office. Brent turns and sees Ben Crawford standing in the door with a double-barreled, 10-gauge shotgun. "The first one of you boys that decides to open the show, I'll blow clear out of his boots."

"You don't want to throw your hat in with him, man." Brent tells Ben. "We aim to kill O'Connor and everyone who helps him."

"Then I guess you'll have to kill me too, but I'll take a couple of you with me." Henry steps out from the post office behind Ben, his rifle held at hip level and pointing right at the group of riders.

"Same goes for me." Sam comes walking up the street with a shotgun in his hands and a pistol shoved into his waist band. "I'll take these two in the back."

Brent Collins shuffles his feet and touches his tongue to his lips. Issac knows too much about the man and his kind to think that they've got him buffaloed, but he can see the man turning the odds over in his mind. Issac and the men backing him may not kill his whole family, but they'll certainly kill most of them, and the law will be after the ones that get away. Issac can see Brent deciding if it is too risky to try and take him here and now, so he speaks up.

"There ain't no reason for you and yours to die here today, Brent. I ain't going with you so, why don't you drop it? You think killing me will bring back your boy? It won't, believe me. You might feel better at first, but the pain doesn't go away, and the killing only brings on pain of its own, for you and for the families of the men you kill."

"This ain't over, O'Connor." Brent turns and motions for his men to mount up. He climbs onto the buckboard and lays his rifle down. "I think we'll stay here in town for a while and see how things go."

The old man snaps the reins over the mules and his buckboard starts moving. The riders fall into place around him with military-like precision. Issac turns with them and watches them ride up the street to the little bunkhouse motel across from the Last Chance Saloon.

"We can't let 'em stay in town, Issac." Henry says, as he steps off the porch of the post office.

"We can't do anything about them being here, according to the law." Issac turns to all of the men and gives them a nod. "I appreciate what you did back there. They had me dead to rights."

"You'd have done the same thing for us, Issac." Ben places his shotgun on his shoulder. "What are you going to do now?"

"I'm going to wait until dark and stir up a little trouble." Issac's grin is broad and mischievous.

"You want any help?" Sam asks.

"No thanks, Sam. It'll be best if you men stay out of if for now." Issac shakes hands with all of them in turn. "And watch out for Deborah for me."

He walks off down the street and disappears into an alley. He lounges around town the rest of the day, listening to the conversations going on to judge what the Collins' are going to do, as they are always hiding in the shadows. As darkness falls upon Jericho, he has a plan formulated, but he isn't sure he can pull it off. Slipping into the back of his wife's store, he finds her at the counter, watching the street. He hurries up to her and explains to her what he is going to do. She doesn't protest, but she hugs him long and hard. Stepping back, he leans down and kisses her hard. She looks up at him, her eyes watery.

"Saddle the roan, put my carbine in the boot, and get me enough food for two weeks. Put a sack of corn in one of the saddlebags for the roan, and make sure you feed him before you tie him up under the bridge. Do you think you can do that without being seen?"

"I can, Issac." She grips his hand. "But do you have to go?"

"Somebody's got to get them out of town or they'll burn it down around us. I know this man's type, and he won't quit. I'll have to take it to him."

Issac slips out of the store through the front door, not wanting to use the same door twice. Having slipped into his moccasins, his feet don't make a sound on the boardwalk. He makes his way up the street toward the Last Chance Saloon. He figures that Brent and the others will be there if they're anywhere.

He walks around to the back of the saloon and listens, trying to determine where everyone is inside, but with all the people talking, it is next to impossible. Stepping into the saloon through the back door, he stands for a second and lets his eyes adjust to the brighter atmosphere of the saloon. He steps around the corner of the bar and locates the Collins' with his eyes. They are all seated together at two tables near the back. Eleven of them. That's everyone. Taking another step, he lets his hand hover above his gun butt. He speaks, as the sound of his voice stops every conversation at once, creating a silence that is deafening.

"Collins." Brent and the others turn to face him. "You wanted trouble, well here it is. I ain't running."

He can see Brent weighing the odds against going for his rifle propped up against the table, but the man's eyes drop down to Issac's pistol. No doubt he's heard stories about how fast he is with a gun. Cain and Abel start to get up and fan out, but Issac stops them cold.

"Cain! Abel! If either one of you gets up from your seats, I'll shoot your dad through the brisket. At this distance I won't miss."

The men settle back down, but their faces flame red with anger. Standing there with his hand above his gun, Issac stares down Brent. The old man wants to kill him, but he's smart enough to know that a move now would mean certain death. Focused on the men in front of him, Issac doesn't see the young man on his right move, but the bartender does and he whispers to Issac.

"Watch it, Issac. He's one of them."

Of course, Issac has time to think. He must be the way that Sam found out about the Collins' in the first place. He turns his head and sees a young man of about 14 reaching for his pistol. Issac doesn't think about how old the boy is; in this harsh land, a gun kills just the same in the hands of a man or child, and the boy has murder in his eyes. Spinning on the balls of his feet, he draws and fires. The boy never stands a chance. The bullet strikes him just above the shirt pocket. He sits down hard, blood frothing from his lips.

"You son of a bitch!" Brent bellows.

Issac hears chairs and boots scraping the floor. Whirling around, he fires at the first man he sees, and the man goes down, clawing at his throat. A bullet screams through by his ear and another burns the side of his neck. He holsters his gun and vaults over the bar, bullets smacking all around him. Landing, he runs for the back door and bursts out into the night. Running lightly along the backs of the businesses, he makes his way for the bridge, the place where Deborah stashed the roan and his supplies.

Yells can be heard from up the street, as he slides down the bank and runs under the bridge. The roan is exactly where he told Deborah to put it. He leaps into the saddle and rides up the bank on the other side. Pulling his pistol, he lets out a yell and fires twice into the air. Shouts from up the street let him know that the men heard him, and he soon hears horses being gathered. Touching his heels to the roan, they light out at a fast gallop. You wanted trouble? Well, let's see how much you like the desert and all the trouble that she can give you. She's a harsh mistress, that I can assure you, boys.

He leans down and pats the eager roan on the neck. The horse wants to run, so he gives him his head, as he reloads his pistol and checks his carbine in the boot. South and west of town lay the Red Rocks, a series of canyons, and farther to the south lay the lava flats, some of the harshest terrain known to man or beast. A place where a man can die not three feet from a water hole without knowing it was there. But Issac knows the land, and plans on giving the Collins family a miserable chase to the Red Rocks.

Issac rides throughout the night, walking his horse at times. By morning, the dust cloud is closing on him, but he knows this country well. He leads them on a merry chase for three days through the desert. Only stopping at night for a couple of hours at a time to water and graze his horse. On the fourth day, he can see that instead of stopping in the night, the men trailing him rode straight through and are almost upon him, but he is close to the canyons and confident that he will reach them before the riders reach him. He can see the riders no more than a mile behind, as he drops off into the canyon. In the middle of the canyon, a small stream runs with a high bank. He drops off into the stream and rides up it. He knows that this won't slow them, but he has a plan.

Up ahead the canyon forks, as does the stream. He rides up the left side about a hundred yards, before turning his horse back and riding up the other fork. He stops at the fork, where he caves some dirt from the bank into the stream to muddy the water. The water is flowing in the direction he is going, so the dirt will be carried down the stream for a long way. He hopes they will think that he caved in the bank on the right for to make them think he went right instead of left.

He rides hard for a small cleft in the rock a few hundred yards ahead. The cleft is actually a switch-back trail that leads out of the canyon. The roan shies from the trail at first, but with a little coaxing it starts up. The trail is so narrow in places that his foot and stirrup scrap the wall, while his other foot hangs out over the ledge. He stops when he's close to the top and takes his field glasses out of his saddle bags. He has cloth wrapped around the end of them to keep them from glaring in the sun. From up here, he has an excellent view of the forks of the canyon, but no one down there couldn't see him unless they were directly below him.

Issac looks through the glasses and sees the riders come to the fork in the stream. One of the men climbs down from his horse and studies the caved-in bank and the floor of the canyon. Straightening up, he points down the left branch and mounts up. The riders take the bait and go down the left branch of the canyon. Issac smiles to himself. Tying the roan to a bunch of mesquite, he walks back down the switch-back trail and covers his horse's tracks. He hurries back up the trail, liking the way his muscles feel as he moves about. He hasn't moved like this in a long time, and it feels good.

Mounting the roan, he rides along the top of the canyon for some ways before cutting to the south away from the canyon, so the riders won't hear him. After a while, he rides back and ties his horse far from the mouth of the canyon. Walking to the edge, careful not to skyline himself, he settles down in the shade of a large boulder, for which he has plans. As he takes a drink of water, he thinks about his next move, but he isn't waiting long.

The riders round the bend in the canyon at a slow pace, each man studying the ground for prints. Issac places his shoulder against the bolder and waits. He lets the first six riders go through before he starts to push. He doesn't want to kill anyone, just spook their horses and scare the men a little. The boulder gives and he redoubles his efforts. The rock gives a groan and rolls over the edge. Issac doesn't wait around to see what happened. He unties the roan and climbs into the saddle. As he turns and heads away from the canyon, he can hear men and horses screaming in pain. You boys wanted trouble. Now you've got it. Just keep on coming if you want more.

Issac rides to a water hole he knows just a few miles from the canyon. He's careful to keep to hard rock and soft sand as much as he can. A couple of javelina are watering when he rides into the small hollow made by up thrust boulders. The look up at him, their snouts dripping water, but walk away, unconcerned by his presence, but not liking the smell of him all the same. Issac waters the roan and fills his canteen. He stakes the roan on some grass far from the water in the shade provided by a huge up-thrust rock, not wanting to disturb the animals that come to use the water hole. Gathering a few sticks and some kindling, he builds a fire that he could cover with his hat, and then boils some coffee. Drinking a scalding hot cup of coffee and chewing on a piece of jerky, he contemplates his next move. He figures that tonight he will hit their camp if he can sneak in close enough.

Issac settles back in the shade of the boulder, and trusting his horse to warn him if anybody tries to come up on him, he drifts off to sleep to the sound of the roan cropping grass. He wakes a few hours later, as the sun is just going down. He builds another small fire and leads the roan to the water hole while the water for his coffee boils. He drinks a quick cup of coffee and mounts his horse. It is completely dark by the time he reaches the lip of the canyon, where he tumbled the boulder down onto the men below. The moon is just bright enough for him to see a dead horse at the bottom, but no bodies. Maybe I didn't kill anyone, but I bet they rode a lot more careful the rest of the way through the canyon. Riding to the mouth the canyon, he finds them almost immediately. The tracks head for a small pool made by the stream that runs along the canyon floor. Circling wide around the pool, he rides up to the backside of Baldy Nob, a hill barely big enough to be considered a mountain.

Tying his horse to a cedar, he takes his field glasses and makes his way up the backside of the mountain. He finds a small outcropping of rock and settles down onto it. Scanning the country below, he picks up his pursuer's fire almost at once. They are camped at the pool, just like he figured they would be. Issac can't quite make out individuals, but he can see movement, so he waits. After an hour or more, the movement begins to cease. Turning in for the night. Now's the time to pay them a little visit. He makes his way carefully back down the hill to his horse and mounts up. Skirting the backside of the mountain, he makes his way to a small hollow a few hundred yards from the men's camp. Using a slip knot, he ties his horse to a clump of mesquite. He ties the roan tight enough to keep him in place, but loose enough that if he whistles the horse will be able to pull loose and come for him.

Issac slips his carbine from the boot and slips out of the hollow, his feet not making any noise in the sand. The camp is just ahead, so he settles down and watches. Two men sit on opposite sides of the fire, talking to each other over cups of coffee. A third man sits, staring out into the night. He carefully counts all 10 men, seven of them already rolled up in their blankets and asleep. Waiting for the two men to turn in, he spots each canteen and commits the location to memory. When the men dump their dredges into the fire, Issac notices that one of them has his arm in a sling. He chuckles lightly to himself. The men lay on their bedrolls and in moments are sleeping soundly. Issac waits and watches the guard, and he eventually does exactly what Issac hopes he would do. When the man adds wood to the fire, he stares at the flames for a moment too long, ruining his night vision.

Working his way to where the horses are tied, he takes out his Bowie knife and cuts the picket line, freeing the horses. He slips around the camp away from the sentry, and using a long stick he found, he goes to work stealing the canteens from the group. Slipping on his belly within a few feet of the fire, but keeping to the shadows, he runs the stick out and carefully winds it around the strap on the canteen. Lifting the canteen, he pulls it back to himself.

It takes him nearly an hour and half to gather six of the 10 canteens, the others are either within the sight of the sentry or too close to a sleeping person for him to risk it. Putting the canteens on his shoulder, careful to not let them clink together, Issac makes his way back to his horse. He places two of the canteens on his pommel and the rest he busts open with a rock. Carefully, he picks his way back to the camp with his carbine in hand. Fifty yards away, he stops and takes aim on the fire. He is on a rise slightly above the camp, so he doesn't think the bullets will ricochet and hit anyone, but then again he really doesn't care. These men are here to kill you and will do so at the drop of a hat. Issac smiles in the darkness as he nestles the carbine against his check. The combination rifle and pistol is light enough for him to shoot with just one hand. It is a little awkward, but after some practice, he is almost as good with it as he ever was with a rifle, not to mention the range is better than a pistol.

With his sights set on the fire, Issac lets two shots go as quick as he can trigger them. Burning sticks and coals jump in every direction, as the bullets slam into the fire. The horses scream and take off into the night, hooves thundering as they run. The sentry jumps up and raises his rifle in Issac's direction, but he calmly shoots the man's hat from his head. The sentry drops and scuttles for cover behind a rock. He busts another canteen with his forth shot and grazes the leg of a man with his fifth. His last shot busts the stock on a rifle left lying in the open. The camp is quiet now that the horses have run off. Issac lifts his voice, as he walks back to his own horse.

"You boys wanted this! Come and get it!"

Putting heels to the roan, he rides for another small pool he knows a few miles west of Baldy Nob. The water hole lies on the side of another mountain called Little Horn, which is among some slabs that have fallen from the mountain. The elevation will be enough that he can watch over the men below and see what their next move will be. He keeps the roan in soft sand and hard rock, switching back now and then to cover his trail. Issac knows this land well, and in no time his trail is a confusing mess of tracks, before it finally disappears completely.

Three hours later, the sun shows itself over the horizon. Issac is tucked under a cedar with his field glasses and a cup of coffee. His horse is picketed behind him, where he will warn Issac if anyone should try to come up that way. Sipping his coffee, he watches the men below, as they go about collecting their horses. The work is long and brutal. The horses are still spooked from the night before, as well as the strangeness of the land. Eventually they get all of the horses rounded up and back to camp. He watches them, as the split up into two groups. The group of six heads north, back to town, while the other four follow his tracks back to where he tied his horse the night before. Looks like you boys just haven't had enough.

Issac has been avoiding the lava field, because he knows what kind of hell they can be in the middle of the day with the sun beating down on you and the black rocks around you, absorbing the heat and making it feel like a furnace. He makes up his mind that if they want to follow, he will give them a chase they won't soon forget. Making sure his canteens are full, he mounts up and rides down the side of the mountains. He rides directly at the group of four.

A hundred yards off, they spot him coming, and someone raises a yell that carries easily in the desert morning air. Issac whirls his horse and points him southwest. Patting him on the neck for good luck, he touches his heels to the roan and they leave out at a run. The roan stretches out beneath him in a ground-eating gate, as bullets whistle through the air and smack the sand around him. He can hear one of the riders behind him yelling for the others to stop shooting. He yells something that sounds like 'Pa wants him alive', but Issac is already almost out of earshot. The roan has been stabled and eating corn for the last few months, so he has plenty of energy to spare. The horses of the men behind him have been traveling hard for the last few weeks and almost immediately start to flag.

Running up a hollow at top speed, Issac heads for the lava flats. Most men avoid the flats. Even the Indians avoided them before the white man settled in this country. Issac knew an old Indian who told him that the lava flats were filled with spirits of men who had died in the desert. While he was never one to take stock in such nonsense, Issac still couldn't deny the eeriness of riding through the up-thrust slabs and razor sharp rocks, where one slip up could mean death. You had to follow the trails in the bottoms. A horse couldn't navigate the ups and downs of the lava beds, and a man trying to cross the razor sharp terrain would have his boots cut to shreds in an hour. You sure didn't want to try to walk in your socks either; it would cut your feet to ribbons, leaving you dying of thirst and blood loss.

Letting his horse have its head, he loses himself in the up-thrusts and wavelike protrusions. A few hours later, he takes a small jaunt across some flat rock to a small water hole he knows about. Watering the roan, he listens carefully for any sign of pursuit. Issac feeds the roan some of the corn his wife packed, and then lets him rest for half an hour before moving on again.

The sun beats down on the land around Issac, turning it into a furnace. Sweat runs freely down his face and chest. His shirt sticks to him and grows wet, but still he rides deeper into the lava flats. His horse sweats, the dust sticking to him and turning his coat brown. But Issac still rides deeper. The men behind him have only their canteens and what water they can find along the way, but he has his canteen and two others. He stops once and gives his horse a drink by filling his hat with water from one of the canteens. The sun begins to set and the cool air rushes in, making him shiver. He continues to ride until he comes to a trail that cuts through the lave fields.

Taking the trail, he soon comes to a small water hole. The pool is almost empty, and the water in the bottom is brackish, but he and the roan drink it greedily, not knowing when they will get another chance to drink. Leaving the roan ground hitched, he climbs a slab of rock with his field glasses and studies his back trail in the dying light. The riders are still behind him, but they don't look good. He can see a bandage on one of the men's legs where he undoubtedly tried to climb an up-thrust of lave and cut himself. These boys are game and they can track, but we'll see how game they are by morning.

The sun dips below the horizon, as Issac mounts his horse. Riding back to the trail his pursuers are on, he rides on, leaving a trail a child could follow. For two days he makes their ride through the lava flats as miserable as he can. On the second day, he bursts out of the lava flats and into the desert. Funny how this can look like heaven after going through that hell back there. Issac puts the roan into a canter and heads across country toward Jericho, which is about 70 miles to the northwest. When he's a few miles from the lava flats, the sun dips below the horizon and he goes to work hiding his trail. He uses every trick he knows. He doubles back on his own trail, hitting soft sand and hard rock, he wraps cloth around the hooves of his horse and takes to a granite ridge that runs north.

Finding a small hollow in a dry river bed, he makes camp for the night, feeding the roan the last of the corn. After he waters his horse, he builds a small fire and makes coffee. As he fries some thick slices of bacon and bread, he drinks the coffee and relishes in its taste. He can feel the food and coffee giving his body strength almost immediately. Thinking about his pursuers, he chuckles. Those boys must be having one hell of a night. As far as I know, they haven't had water for three days. Their horses have got to be on their last legs. Issac rolls up in his bed and turns in for the night, trusting the roan to warn him if anyone comes too close during the night.

He wakes to the sound of the roan stomping its hooves and snorting quietly. The fire has burnt down to coals, but still give off some light. Grabbing for his carbine, Issac leaves his blankets immediately and dives for the shadow of a boulder a few feet away. He studies his surroundings for a moment, his ears straining for any sound. Gunfire erupts in the night. Bullets strike again and again into his blankets, where he was only moment before. Two men step into the dying light of the fire, their guns trained on his bedroll. Damn those boys can track, Issac thinks to himself, but a good look at the men approaching his bedroll reveals that they aren't the same ones that followed him through the lave fields. They are part of the group that split off from the rest nearly four days ago.

You're in trouble, Issac. They didn't all go into Jericho. Some of them circled around and headed you off.

The men reach his bedroll, as Issac makes his move. Leaping from the shadow of the boulder, he fires the carbine into the chest of the man closest to him, watching him go down hard. Firing again at the other man, he sees him turn from the impact of the bullet. Bullets rake the camp, scattering coals everywhere as they strike the fire. Running flat out, he drops the carbine when a bullet burns the back of his hand.

Leaping on the roan, he rides him bareback out of the hollow and up the side of the dry river bed. Bullets swarm through the air around him. The roan makes the top of the bank and stretches out to run. On the second leap, the roan's front hoof finds a goffer hole, causing him to go head over heels with a scream. Issac is thrown from the saddle. As the ground rushes up at him, he has time to think, we gave 'em one hell of a chase before they got us. He hits hard on his shoulder and then tucks and rolls with the momentum.

He comes up fast with his gun in his hand. He can just make out a couple of riders closing in on him. Issac lets the rider in the lead have a slug from his pistol to the stomach. The man in the lead stands up in his stirrups and pitches off his horse to the side. Issac brings his pistol to bear on the second rider, his feet spread wide, a grimace on his bleeding face. Something hot hits him on the side of the head and his knees give way. This is it. You just got shot in the head. Deborah, I'm sorry. Blackness takes him, as the ground rushes up to meet his face.

~~~

A man dressed in a neatly-pressed suit steps down from the stage and whips the dust from his body with his bowler's hat. The silver band on the hat flashes brightly in the noon sunlight. He doesn't appear to be wearing a gun, something that is almost unheard of in the West. He reaches back inside the stage and grabs a long, black bag. Hoisting the bag on his shoulder, the man makes his way to the Emporium. Inside, he buys a room and goes upstairs. The name he writes on the directory is Douglas Harlow. When he comes back down, he is barely noticeable as the same man who went up. He now wears a black, button-up shirt and black jeans instead of a suit. He has traded his bowler's hat for a wide-brimmed, flat-crowned black hat. Twin tied-down holsters of black leather adorn his hips. The flashy pearl-handled guns in the holsters seem to defy the rest of the man's drab clothing.

Striding out of the Emporium, Douglas takes a second to stand on the porch and orient himself. He spies the jailhouse and starts toward it. The sound of horses stops him, as he melts into the shadows of an alley between buildings. Four dusty and haggard looking men ride up the street and head straight for the Last Chance Saloon. The older man at the front of the column is obviously the leader, but Douglas has eyes only for the two behind him. Impossibly tall and thin, he knows their kind by sight. They've killed a few men and fancy themselves as gunfighters and all around bad men, but he's seen boys like them come and go. Most of them are pushing up daisies on Boot Hill now.

He almost steps from the shadows and calls out to them, but something makes him stop. Instead, he watches them ride up to the saloon and dismount. When they disappear inside, he walks on over to the jailhouse and steps inside. Henry's chair thumps the floor, and as Douglas enters, the Sheriff sets up to greet him.

"Howdy, stranger. Something I can do for you?"

"Hello, Sheriff. There certainly is something that you can do for me." Douglas gestures toward the street. "Where is Issac O'Connor?"

Henry's eyes take on a weird light and his hand inches a little closer to the shotgun laying on the corner of his desk. He looks the stranger up and down, but he can't bring himself to be suspicious of the man. Something about him makes Henry like him instantly.

"What do you want with Issac?"

"I'm his cousin, Douglas Harlow." Douglas strides over to Henry's desk and holds out a hand.

Henry takes the offered hand. "Issac road out of town a week or so ago with the Collins' on his heels. His wife said something about him taking them through the lava flats when I asked her where he was going, but she didn't know anymore."

"Ilza died years ago." Douglas looks at the Sheriff, with a confused expression on his face.

"Not Ilza. Deborah, his new wife." Henry shakes his head sadly. "He married her after his daughter was killed and he lost his right arm to the Irons' Gang. She doctored him when he was down and out."

"I see." Douglas gestures again toward the saloon up the street. "Those men who just road into town. Are they part of the Collins' family?"

"You bet your bottom dollar they are. The old man in the lead is Brent's brother, Caleb. Brent is the leader of the clan. Those two behind him are Jeb and Dalton, Caleb's boys, and they're hell on wheels, but they ain't nowhere as good as Brent's boys..."

"Cain and Abel." Douglas finishes for him.

"Sure. How'd you know that?"

"Me and Issac had trouble with them back in Missouri before I moved out West. How many of them are there?"

"There were 12, but Issac killed two of them before he left town." Henry explains.

"Thanks, Sheriff. I think I'll go and have myself a little talk with those boys and see if they know where Issac is."

Douglas turns and starts for the door.

"Do you need any help?"

"I appreciate that, Sheriff, but I think you better sit this one out."

With that, Douglas steps out into the street and heads towards the saloon. Tenpenny music comes from a music box inside, as he steps up to the batwing doors. He steps through the door and to the side, letting his eyes adjust to the lighting inside the saloon. The air inside the saloon is much cooler than the midday heat outside. The music box rambles some tune in the corner. A woman's laughter drifts down from upstairs. The four men who rode into town are sitting at the bar with drinks in their hands. Three older men sit at a table to his left playing poker, and a couple more, cowhands by the look of their clothes, are sitting at a table talking to a couple of girls dressed in glimmering gowns that leave little to the imagination. The bartender sees him when he walks in, and lays his hairy arms on the bar.

"You want a drink or a meal, stranger?"

"Neither my good man." Douglas steps to the side, putting himself in line with the Jeb and

Dalton. "I'm here for Issac O'Connor."

The men at the bar stiffen, as if they just had cold water poured down their backs. Caleb turns around, mug in his hand, and looks Douglas up and down, his eyes resting for a moment on the twin tie-downs. Jeb and Dalton do the same, but they hold their beers in their left hands, their right hands rest on their thighs. The fourth man, a boy really, turns around, but his face grows pale when he sees the tied-down guns on Douglas' hips, and he swallows hard. The older man speaks first.

"What do you want with Issac?"

"My name is Douglas Harlow. I'm his kin, and he asked for my help." Douglas grins at the men. "It seems that a bunch of low-down, yellow-bellied cowards are dogging him and he needs a little backing."

The faces of the men at the bar turn bright red at being called cowards, but no one makes a move, yet. Jeb and Dalton step off their stools and set their beers on the bar, their eyes never leaving Douglas.

"You best take that back, mister." The man on the right speaks slowly.

"I won't. Any man who would attack a crippled man with 12 men is a coward."

"I'm warning you, mister."

"Do your warning, son. I've done made up my mind. The way I see it, you boys have two options facing you. You can ride out now. I'll give you three minutes to collect your gear. Or you can stay and die. Either way, makes no difference to me, but I surely do hate to kill a man when I just get into a town."

"I don't know who you are, mister, but you swing a pretty wide loop. I don't think you've got the sand to stand against us."

"Just let your dogs bark, son, and I'll show you what hand I'm holding."

Jeb and Dalton turn to their father. Caleb studies Douglas for moment and nods his head. He steps away from the bar and speaks.

"Go ahead, boys. Show him some manners."

He looks up at Douglas with a nasty smile on his face. "You wanted 'em, mister, well now you've got 'em."

Jeb and Dalton step off their stools and take a few steps apart. Douglas watches them with lazy eyes. He has seen this routine before and hates the fact that these boys are about to be dead. A damned shame is what it is. These boys aren't cut out for the West. They should be back East, farming and raising a family, but now they'll get an unmarked grave in a small town in the middle of nowhere. Douglas lets his hands dangle beside his gun butts.

Jeb's head thrusts forward, as his hand drops for his gun. Dalton takes a quick step to the left, hoping to throw off Douglas, as he reaches for his own gun. Neither of the Collins' guns clear leather before his guns roar loudly in the saloon. A woman shrieks upstairs, as the saloon is otherwise quiet except for the gasping of Jeb, as he slumps against the bar clawing at a hole in his throat. Dalton lies on the floor with a perfect hole between his eyes. Douglas starts to shift his guns to the other men when Caleb speaks from his left.

"You kilt my boys, mister." The sound of the hammer being cocked on his rifle is quite loud in the quiet saloon. "Drop them guns to the ground and do it fast."

Douglas lets his guns fall from his hands. Out of the corner of his eye, he can see the other boy at the bar, his eyes wide and staring at the dead men who were his kin. He raises his hands to shoulder height, as he turns to face Caleb.

"I'm gonna kill you now, mister."

"I'm sure you think that, but the fact is . . . "

Douglas' right hand blurs toward his collar, as he grips the knife he keeps in a sheath down his back. His arm whips forward, sending the knife end over end through the air to bury to the hilt in the older man's throat, just above his collar bone. Caleb's rifle discharges into the floor, the boom loud in the saloon. The man drops his gun and tries to pull the knife from his throat, but only succeeds in making the wound worse. He falls to the floor in a growing pool of his own blood. Douglas dips down and scoops up his guns. Training them on the boy at the bar, who is still standing there with his eyes wide, he speaks.

"Don't make me kill you too, son. Unbuckle your gun belt and let it fall."

The boy complies, but his eyes never leave his dying father on the floor. When he speaks, his voice is incredulous, "You killed my Pa and brothers, mister."

"Yes, I did, but they were asking for it, son." Douglas holsters his guns and retrieves his knife from Caleb's throat. He wipes the blade off on the man's clothes. "Now you and I are going over to the Sheriff's, and we're going to have a good, long talk."

When Douglas is gone, one of the men at the poker table goes and gets the undertaker. The other men just gradually drift together to talk about the events that just took place, as men will do given the chance. One of the cowhands speaks what they are all thinking.

"Who in the world was that?"

The bartender puts the mug he was cleaning under the bar and drops his rag on the top of the bar. He looks from one man to the other, as he leans his hairy forearms on the bar.

"That, gentlemen, was King O'Hara."

"You're kidding." One of the men playing poker laughs. "King O'Hara and his partner Jamie Grey were the fastest men with guns since Wes Hardin and Bill Longley."

"That was him all right. I saw him and his partner a long time ago in Missouri when he had a run in with the Bald Nobbers."

"I wonder what happened to Jamie Grey?"

The bartender smiles, as if he knows some inside joke that the others don't, before he answers.

"I figure he's either dead or he did the same thing that King did: changed his name and quit outlawing before he was dead."

"I'll be a son of a gun." The cowhand who asked who the man was takes of his hat and wipes his brow with the back of his hand. "With King

O'Hara here, those Collins boys better light out while they can."

"You sure ain't kidding." His buddy agrees and turns to the bar. "How about another beer and then we'll help you with those bodies there."

"Sure thing, boys. This one's on the house."

~ ~ ~

Issac awakes to cold water being splashed on his face. His head is beating like a drum and his mouth tastes like copper. He tries to move, but he is tied to a tree. Opening his eyes, he looks right into the face of Cain Collins. The grin on the man's face is an evil one. Brent, Abel, and two other men sit around the camp staring at him with equally malicious grins on their faces. Issac studies the sky for a moment, and judging by the stars, he determines that he has been out for at least a couple of hours, possibly more. He remembers the roan going down, and feels a pang of hurt for the horse. He was a damned good animal. Studying the terrain, he realizes that they have him tied to a cottonwood in the stand along the Snakeskin, just a couple of miles outside of Jericho. Funny it should wind up here again. He knows that he is going to die here. They've got him at their mercy. Most people would plead and beg for their life, but it just isn't in him to do such a thing. Instead, he feels that old Viking berserk rising inside of him. Issac looks up into the eyes of Brent, and speaks, "Looks like you're a few boys short, Brent."

"Perhaps I am, but you're fixing to lose your hide, O'Connor."

"Was it worth it? Just to kill one man." Issac stares around the camp and wonders where the other four men are.

"You kilt our kin. A man can't let something like that go."

"He was running with a band of outlaws that killed my daughter, Collins. I gave him a chance to run, but he stuck with 'em. He chose to throw in with a bad crowd and was killed for it."

"Makes no difference, O'Connor. You're gonna die here just the same" Brent gives him a smile and gestures around the camp at the others. "But first, we're gonna have us some fun."

Issac knew the Collins' back in Missouri, where he had a run in with their kin fighting the Bald Nobbers. He knew then that Brent had a mean streak in him, but looking in the eyes of the man and the others around him, he can see that it is more than just a mean streak, it is some kind of sickness of the mind. A sickness that draws them to hurting and killing.

"You fancy yourself good with a gun, don't you? Well, Cain and Abel here are gonna show you how good they are."

Cain and Abel walk to the edge of the camp and then turn. Cain moves his bottom lip, as both men palm their guns in the same instant. That's how they throw you off. Cain gives the command and they draw at the same time. A bullet burns along Issac's cheek and another tears a gash along his right shoulder. He doesn't want to give them the satisfaction of seeing him in pain, so he grits his teeth and holds still, as bullets smack the tree all around him. One tears the end off of his moccasin, making his toes hurt, making him hope that they didn't shoot off his toes. I'll have a hell of a time walking without my toes. He thinks. What are you talking about you fool. You're gonna die right here under this tree. You won't have to worry about walking when they've got you swinging at the business end of a rope. Finally, the twins run out of bullets and step back into camp, laughing to each other. Brent stands and gathers his rifle. In one smooth motion, he raises it and fires. Issac sees the flame belch forth and knows that he is dead.

The bullet tears away a piece of his left ear in a spray of blood.

"You're not the only one who can shoot, O'Connor. Just thought we'd let you know that before we commence to putting the hurt on you." Brent reaches into his back pocket and pulls out a pair of pliers, opening and closing them in front of his face. "Now you're gonna lose some toenails."

One of the other men that Issac doesn't know walks up to Brent and touches his shoulder. Issac breathes a small sigh of relief. He doesn't know how badly it's going to hurt to have his toenails pulled, but he is sure he isn't going to enjoy it. He watches them talk, as blood runs from a half a dozen wounds over his body.

"The others have sure been gone a long time, Pa."

"What?"

"Uncle Caleb and the others. They've sure been gone a long time. They left this morning and they still ain't back. Close as we are to town, they should have been back hours ago, even if they got to drinking in town."

"He's right, Pa." Abel speaks up from where he lounges on his bedroll.

Brent looks around for a moment, as if just noticing where he is, and his face softens. "You're right, boys. Cain, Abel, you two ride into town and see about Caleb and the others. If they got themselves into trouble with the local authorities and you can get 'em out, do it, but if it looks too bad, you get yourselves back here and we'll go into town in force and burn that son of a bitch down around their ears. Got it?"

"Sure, Pa. Come on, Abel."

The two men swiftly saddle their horses, and in moments they're on the trail for Jericho. Issac listens to the retreating sound of their horse's hooves and knows that he has until the time they get back to live. Brent will want the whole family together for the hanging. Trying to think of a way out of his predicament, he comes up with nothing. Brent looks back at him with a malicious grin on his face, and speaks.

"We'll have to wait a little while for the real fun, but until those boys get back we can have a little ourselves." He opens and closes the pliers.

Brent walks over and pulls off Issac's left moccasin, the one that Cain had shot. With a chuckle, the man bends down and grips his big toenail with the pliers, giving the pliers a little tug. Issac does his best to not show the pain; he doesn't want to give them the satisfaction. Brent looks up with a smile, but when he sees that Issac is looking down at him with a look of anger and hate rather than hurt and pleading, his smile fades. Bending back down, he tears the toenail off with one quick jerk. Shifting the pliers, he does the same to the next toe, and then the next in quick succession with two quick pulls.

Pain blossoms in each toe, white-hot pain that radiates through his foot and up his leg. Air whistles through Issac's gritted teeth, but otherwise he gives them no indication that he is hurting. Working slowly, Brent pulls the other two nails off of his foot, as the other men look on and laugh. Brent starts to take his other moccasin off, but the sound of guns being cocked stops him. A voice speaks from the darkness outside of the camp.

"Drop those pliers, Brent, and step back."

One of the two men on the other side of the fire make like he is going for his gun. A gun roars in the night, and a bullet kicks sand into the man's face, as it strikes within inches of his hand. Both men settle back into their bedrolls.

"Any more fool moves like that and I'll shoot both of you on principal. Brent, take that knife out of your belt and throw it away."

Issac sees Brent wondering if he can kill him with the knife before the stranger could kill him, but he complies and throws the knife away. Must be thinking that Cain and Abel and the others will be back soon enough. Issac speaks up so the man in the darkness can hear him.

"I don't know who you are, mister, but they've got four more men in town and another two headed that way. Jericho ain't far so; they'll be back in no time."

The man steps into the fire light with his pearl-handled guns trained on Brent and the other men. The man gestures with his gun, as Brent joins the other two men on the other side of the fire. Douglas walks around the tree, keeping his right-hand gun on the men, while holstering his other gun. He draws a knife, and working carefully but quickly, he cuts Issac loose.

Issac's arm and legs arm numb. He stumbles, but he manages to keep his hold on the tree.

Working his hand to get the circulation back, he speaks to Douglas.

"I sure am glad to see you, Douglas, but we've got to hurry; those others will be back anytime."

Douglas smiles. "Maybe the two who left this camp will, but the four in town won't. I killed three of them and the fourth is sitting in a jail cell as we speak."

"You son of a bitch. That was my Pa." One of the men sitting by Brent screams, his voice shrill with pain and anger. He dives for his gun. The camp explodes. Brent rolls to the side and grabs his rifle, as the other man drops his hand for his pistol. In one smooth motion, one the two cousins used to practice when they were younger, Douglas draws his left-hand gun and border shifts it to Issac, who catches the gun.

Concentrating on Brent, Issac fires twice. The older man jerks and drops his rifle when the first shot hits him. The second strikes him between the eyes, causing his knees to buckle and sending him face first into the sand. Issac turns and fires at the man holding a pistol. The man jerks, as both Issac and Douglas' bullets hit him in the chest. His pistol goes off as he dies, but the bullet goes wide. The men watch for any other movement, but all is quiet.

Issac turns to Douglas and hands him back his gun.

"I sure am glad to see you, King." He smiles.

"Don't call me that, Issac." Douglas takes the gun and reloads the spent cartridges. "You know I dropped that name years ago."

"I know, Douglas." Issac gives him a slap on the back, and walks over to his gun belt.

Douglas watches Issac strap on his gun belt and holster his pistol. He takes the other and shoves it into his waist band. Douglas looks the man up and down, shaking his head. Where a young man would have once stood, an old man now fills his shoes.

"You look like you've been through it the last few years, Issac." Douglas shakes his head. "The

Sheriff told me about Abigail. I'm sorry Issac. She was a good girl."

"She sure was."

"Sheriff also said that you got married again."

"I did." Issac grins. "She is a hell of a woman, Douglas. A woman to stand beside a man."

"I'm glad, Issac." Douglas gestures toward Jericho with a jerk of his head. "What do you say we ride into town and finish this? I brought you a horse from your own corral. Deborah said you liked the dun the best besides the roan."

"All right, Douglas. Let's do it."

Issac takes time to gather his moccasin and put it on. It hurts his toes like something fierce, but he pulls it on just the same. He finds his carbine, a good rifle that he'd hate to get rid of, and gathers it up as well. Walking with Douglas to the horses he has stashed in the cottonwoods a few hundred yards away, Issac explains how he lost his arm to a shotgun blast from the same woman who killed Abigail. Douglas tells him what went down in the saloon. He tells him how the boy was more than eager to talk when he took him to the jailhouse and started talking to the Sheriff about building a gallows in the morning to hang him. They find the horses in moments, and the dun nickers when it smells Issac. He rubs the dun's nose, and climbs into the saddle. Shoving his carbine into the boot, he whirls the horse for Jericho, putting his heels to the dun's flanks.

The dun takes a leap, as it stretches out to run. Douglas gives a yell and hits the trail right behind Issac. Five minutes later, they come into town at a dead run, only to see Issac's house is on fire. He leaps from his horse without stopping, and makes a run for the burning house. Douglas just has time to catch him before he makes the porch. The house is a roaring inferno.

"You can't go in there, man." Douglas holds Issac as he struggles.

"Deborah's in there, Douglas. I can't lose her too. I can't."

People are standing around with buckets of water, but they know that the house is long gone. They're just here to keep the fire from spreading to the other houses and businesses. Henry comes across the bridge, and helps Douglas restrain Issac. He finally calms down, but he never takes his eyes off the inferno that used to be his house.

"That Cain and Abel did it. Sam saw 'em ride over to the Last Chance Saloon. They weren't inside no time before they come out and hit their horses. They rode out of town all hell bent for leather, but on the way, they must have lit your house. By the time we got here, the flames were already too high for anyone to get in. I'm sorry, Issac."

"We gotta find 'em, Douglas."

"All right, Issac. Let's rest a bit and we'll be on their trail by first light."

"NO! Right now!"

Issac turns for his horse, but a yell from the bridge stops him.

"O'CONNOR!"

Issac spins on the balls of his feet, and sees Cain and Abel standing in the middle of the bridge with Deborah in front of them. Her hands are tied and she is gagged, but she doesn't seem to be any worse for wear. Without thinking, Issac speaks over his shoulder and starts up the street toward the twins.

"I've got this, Douglas."

"You sure, Issac?" Douglas knows how fast the two men are, and he knows how fast Issac is, or at least how fast he was when he was a younger man. "There's two of them."

"I said I've got it. Stay out."

Issac strides up the street, a look of determination mixed with hate and fury on his face. His hand hovers just above his gun butt, as he stops 40 feet from the two men. The glow from his burning house almost makes the bridge as bright as if it were daylight. Issac raises his voice so he can be heard over the crackling and burning timber of his house.

"Let her go, boys!" Issac takes a few more steps toward them, bringing himself within 30 feet of the two men.

"We'll let her go when you let our Saul go!" Cain yells back.

"It's over, boys! You're pa's dead, along with the rest of your family! Pack it in while you can or you'll be dead along with 'em!"

"Like hell, O'Connor! You've ruined our family, and now we aim to ruin you!"

Abel shoves Deborah to the side, and she goes over the railing of the bridge. Issac watches her go, but right now he knows that he can't do anything more for her than kill these two men in front of him. He watches them closely, as they spread out as far apart as the bridge will let them. He sees Cain's mouth move, as they go for their guns.

Issac's hand is a blur of motion, as his gun clears leather. His first shot hits Cain in the stomach, hitting him before the man can even clear leather. Cain stumbles, but he brings his gun up. Issac fires three more shots in rapid succession, and all three hit Cain in the chest. The gunman drops to his knees, his right-hand gun falling from his grasp. Issac turns just in time to see Abel's gun go off a second time, as the first shot was too hastily taken and went wild. The slug takes Issac in the side, but he raises his gun and fires into the man's chest, once and then again. Abel stumbles back against the railing of the bridge, but his guns keep coming up. A slug hits Issac in the leg, but he keeps his feet by sheer will alone.

Dropping his gun, Issac palms his other pistol. But Abel is still game, as he pushes off of the rail and brings his guns to bear on the man rushing him. Running straight at Abel, Issac fires four more times as fast as he can slip his thumb off of the hammer. The bullets all hit the tall gunman in the chest. The impact of the slugs knock Abel back into the railing, which then gives way, spilling him into the streambed below. Something hot grazes Issac's inner thigh, as he turns to see Cain on his feet. Swaying on his feet with his gun in both hands and blood frothing on his lips, the man fires again, but the shot goes wild. Issac rushes him, firing multiple times. The bullets both hit Cain in the chest, but the man won't go down. Issac sidesteps, circling the gunman, making him turn and keeping him off balance, as he shoves his gun into his waist band and reloads. Cain raises his gun, but Issac walks over to him and kicks it from his hand.

Issac places his gun against the tall gunman's forehead, and thumbs the hammer back. Cain looks up at him with his tongue hanging out and blood frothing from his nostrils and mouth. In that moment, Issac can almost feel sorry for him, but he pulls the trigger nonetheless. The gun bucks in his hand, and Cain slumps to the bridge. Holstering his gun, Issac makes a run for the end of the bridge and around the railing. Sliding down the bank, he yells for Deborah. A muted mumbling, barely audible over the roar of his burning house, answers him. He can hear Douglas and Henry calling for him, but he only has Deborah on his mind. He follows the sound of the muted mumbling, and finds her on her back in the edge of the streambed. Grabbing his knife, he cuts her bonds and pulls the handkerchief from her mouth. She leaps up and hugs him tight around the neck. Issac hugs her back, as tightly as he can.

Deborah sobs into his shoulder for a long time, as Douglas and Henry make their way down the bank to them. Issac gives them a nod, as they walk over to Abel and make sure he's really dead, and sure enough, he is. If the bullets didn't kill him, the way he landed on his head did. Issac pulls back from Deborah and starts to tell her that he loves her, but blackness takes him.

~~~

Issac wakes in a white-walled room that has white curtains, a setting that is all too familiar to him, although he isn't sure how he got here. Looking around, he doesn't see anyone else in the room. Sitting up on the edge of the bed makes his head spin a little. He throws back the covers, and sees bandages on his right leg, torso, one on his shoulders, and the foot where Brent Collins pulled his toenails. Moving about must have caused some commotion, as Deborah rushes through the door with a frown on her face.

"You shouldn't be up, Issac."

He laughs and grabs her around the waist. Pulling her down on the bed, he kisses her hungrily. She kisses him back, and for a moment they melt into each other. A cough from the doorway breaks them apart, with Deborah blushing bright red and breathing heavily. She sits in a chair beside the bed, as she fixes her hair. Issac turns to the doorway and sees Douglas standing there, his thumbs hooked in his belt, and a smile on his face.

"Do you kids need some privacy?"

"It would be nice, you snoop." Both men laugh heartily. "I can't tell you how much I appreciate what you have done for me, King." Issac uses the wrong name out of habit.

"I thought his name was Douglas." Deborah questions.

"It is, Debbie. I used to be known by that name a long time ago, but I decided I didn't like it anymore." Douglas looks at Issac and smiles. "This old man here just gets confused sometimes.

Don't you, old man?"

"Sure do, Douglas." Issac smiles. "Thank you, Douglas. I'll never be able to repay you for what you've done for me."

"Don't mention it, Issac."

"What will you do now? Head back to San Francisco?"

"No. I've had enough of the cities to do me for a lifetime. Debbie was informing me that a certain man was killed not too long ago who owned a piece of land to the south. I think I might just lay a claim on that land and run myself a few horses, and maybe some cattle. If there was someone who wanted to go into business with me that is."

Deborah is looking at Issac with innocent eyes, but he can see the eagerness behind them.

"You two set this up huh?" Issac pats his wife on the leg. "All right. I think I have worked enough. It's time for me to sit on a porch for the rest of my days growing fat and lazy."

"You'll do no such thing." Deborah scolds.

Issac and Douglas share a laugh. Deborah holds out for a moment, but joins in too. Douglas leaves, as Doc White comes in and checks on Issac's bandages. When he leaves, Issac turns to Deborah. She gives him a kiss.

"I love you so much, Debbie."

"I love you too, Issac."

"What did Douglas mean that his name used to be King, but he got tired of it?"

"He is King O'Hara, honey."

Deborah's hands come up to her mouth, as she gasps. Issac laughs and takes her hand.

"How do you two know each other? I thought he was an outlaw from Missouri and Kansas? My husband used to talk about how him and his partner, Trent Grey, were the fastest outlaws with guns that ever walked the face of the earth."

Issac looks her directly in the eyes and speaks three words.

"We were, Debbie."

She looks at him for a moment, her face blank. Issac fears that she hasn't taken his revelation well. She looks down, and when she looks back up she is smiling. She wraps him in a hug and holds him tight.

"I don't care about that, Issac."

"I'm never going to let you go, Debbie."

Titles in the series